THE BLOCK

THE
BLOCK

Collage by
ROMARE BEARDEN

Poems by
LANGSTON HUGHES

Selected by Lowery S. Sims and Daisy Murray Voigt

Introduction by
BILL COSBY

The Metropolitan Museum of Art · Viking, New York

VIKING
First published in 1995 by
The Metropolitan Museum of Art, New York,
and Viking, a division of Penguin Books USA Inc.,
375 Hudson Street, New York, New York, 10014, U.S.A.
and Penguin Books Canada Ltd.,
10 Alcorn Avenue, Toronto, Ontario, Canada M4V 3B2.

The illustrations in this book and on the cover and the jacket are details from *The Block,* 1971, by Romare Bearden, American, 1911–1988. Cut-and-pasted papers on Masonite; six panels 49 x 36 inches each, overall size 4 x 18 feet. The Metropolitan Museum of Art, Gift of Mr. and Mrs. Samuel Shore, 1978 (1978.61.1–6). The full image appears on the title page.

Produced with the cooperation of the Estate of Romare Bearden
and Nanette Rohan Bearden.

Grateful acknowledgment is made to Alfred A. Knopf Inc. for permission to reprint the poems by Langston Hughes. "Theme for English B," "Projection," "As Befits a Man," "Juke Box Love Song," "Testimonial," "Note on Commercial Theatre," from *Selected Poems* by Langston Hughes. Copyright ©1959 by Langston Hughes. Reprinted by permission of Alfred A. Knopf Inc. "Late Last Night" from *One-Way Ticket* by Langston Hughes. Copyright 1948 by Alfred A. Knopf Inc. Reprinted by permission of the publisher. "Madam's Calling Cards" from *Selected Poems* by Langston Hughes. Copyright 1948 by Alfred A. Knopf Inc. Reprinted by permission of the publisher. "Harlem Night Song" from *Selected Poems* by Langston Hughes. Copyright 1926 by Alfred A. Knopf Inc. and renewed 1954 by Langston Hughes.. Reprinted by permission of the publisher. "To Be Somebody" from *Selected Poems* by Langston Hughes. Copyright 1950 by Langston Hughes. Reprinted by permission of Alfred A. Knopf Inc. "Corner Meeting" and "Motto" from *The Panther and the Lash* by Langston Hughes. Copyright 1951 by Langston Hughes. Reprinted by permission of Alfred A. Knopf Inc. "Stars" from *Selected Poems* by Langston Hughes. Copyright ©1947 by Langston Hughes. Reprinted by permission of Alfred A. Knopf Inc.

Photograph of Romare Bearden on p. 30 by Peter Polymenakos/TIME Magazine.
Photograph of Langston Hughes on p. 31 by Henry Grossman.
All other photography by The Metropolitan Museum of Art Photograph Studio.

LIBRARY OF CONGRESS CATALOGING-IN-PUBLICATION DATA
Hughes, Langston, 1902–1967.
The block : poems / by Langston Hughes ; collage by Romare Bearden.
p. cm.
Summary : A collection of thirteen of Langston Hughes' poems on African American themes.
ISBN: 0-87099-741-6 (MMA)
ISBN: 0-670-86501-X (Viking)
1. Afro-Americans—Juvenile poetry. 2. City and town life—United States—
Juvenile poetry. 3. Children's poetry, American. [1. Afro-Americans—Poetry.
2. City and town life—Poetry. 3. American poetry.] I. Bearden, Romare,
1911–1988, ill. II. Title.
PS3515.U274B6 1995
811'.52—dc20
95-12336
CIP
AC

Produced by the Department of Special Publications,
The Metropolitan Museum of Art
Design by Raymond P. Hooper

Printed in Singapore

1 3 5 7 9 10 8 6 4 2

INTRODUCTION

I do not recall when I first discovered Romare Bearden and his art. Perhaps it was during the early 1960s when my wife, Camille, and I began collecting the work of Bearden's good friend, Charles White. As a child growing up in the inner city, I had seen many of the masterpieces of Western art by painters like Matisse, Picasso, and Renoir at the Philadelphia Museum of Art. But there were few works by African-American artists in museums in those days. Seeing a work of art like Bearden's *The Block* would have interested me greatly. I lived in a neighborhood very much like the one depicted in Bearden's collage.

I want to share with you some of the reasons why I would have been drawn to this collage. First, the subject that Bearden chose to depict, the block, was very familiar to me and to all who have grown up in the inner cities of our nation. I would surely have been moved, as I am today, by the magic of Bearden's art and by the emotions that the images and the colors evoke. And, the real-life experiences each viewer brings to the work make for a highly personal visit. *The Block* reminds many viewers of people and events from their own lives, and it encourages others to visualize what life might have been like in a busy and exciting Harlem neighborhood.

Using a vivid imagination and memories of his own experiences of maturing to adulthood in Harlem, Bearden presents us with an insightful look at the basic unit within the American city. The block is where children spend a great deal of time learning to socialize and to transact business, be it buying goods at the corner store or simply hanging out with friends from the neighborhood. The block becomes its own community. Some people are born there and choose to remain there throughout their lives. It is a place where the rituals of life occur and also where lessons about life beyond our own community are learned. The homes above the storefront church, the barbershop, encounters on the sidewalk, views through windows, all of the scenes and activities that we associate with urban life are a vital part of Bearden's block. This block will be of particular interest to anyone who has visited Harlem, but it is also a universal place, a recognizable and familiar environment for many people from around the world.

If Bearden shows us the sights, then Langston Hughes gives us the sounds. Street noise and sermons, courting and complaining, rumors and reveries—they are all echoed in these poems of city life. The voices, too, are familiar. They remind us of our neighbors, our teachers, our friends. Hughes captures the sounds of the street and turns them into music. That music is echoed in Bearden's collage. The image of the storefront church evokes sounds of people singing Negro spirituals, Southern hymns, and gospel songs. These everyday sounds blend harmoniously with the rhythmic blues that might be sung and heard in a local club. And these songs are matched with the creative sounds of jazz musicians parading in the streets of Harlem. As we look and read, all these sounds come into our heads, sounds that resound like the thud of a bass drum.

Bearden also provides us with a new way of looking at a work of art. We experience *The Block* through a series of events, almost as though we were watching a movie. In a sequence of scenes, people congregate at the barbershop, at the grocery store, at church, and even at a funeral parlor, and life in all of its myriad forms is paraded before us. This then is the artist's dream, one and the same with that of the filmmaker, who rolls scene after scene before our eyes. In Bearden's hands, collage proves to be a fine medium in which to arrange and rearrange the images of our past and present experiences. When the artist cuts each piece of paper and places it beside another, he purposefully brings unity and clarity to the composition in his own creative language. In a way, art permits us to relive a given moment through our own experience as well as through the creative imagination of the artist.

But most importantly, the poems and the collage in this book present people in all of the ways that we might see them in real life on one of the busy streets of Harlem. It could all be happening today. These pictures and words remind us that artists help us recall past images, ideas, and events or help us to envision worlds that we have never known. At the same time, art helps us become aware of the talents we all have, if we can just use our imagination.

Bearden's collage and Hughes's poems bring us face to face with the roots of our own individual memories or dreams, many of which hark back to life on a particular city block. Do allow yourself the joy of recollecting—or inventing—the many events that take place in an urban neighborhood when you read this handsome book. Read it with imagination and with creative inquiry. Above all, enjoy your stroll down the street as you read this exciting view of *The Block*.

BILL COSBY

THEME FOR ENGLISH B

he instructor said,

> *Go home and write*
> *a page tonight.*
> *And let that page come out of you—*
> *Then, it will be true.*

I wonder if it's that simple?
I am twenty-two, colored, born in Winston-Salem.
I went to school there, then Durham, then here
to this college on the hill above Harlem.
I am the only colored student in my class.
The steps from the hill lead down into Harlem,
through a park, then I cross St. Nicholas,
Eighth Avenue, Seventh, and I come to the Y,
the Harlem Branch Y, where I take the elevator
up to my room, sit down, and write this page:

It's not easy to know what is true for you or me
at twenty-two, my age. But I guess I'm what
I feel and see and hear, Harlem, I hear you:
hear you, hear me—we two—you, me, talk on this page.
(I hear New York, too.) Me—who?
Well, I like to eat, sleep, drink, and be in love.
I like to work, read, learn, and understand life.
I like a pipe for a Christmas present,
or records—Bessie, bop, or Bach.
I guess being colored doesn't make me *not* like
the same things other folks like who are other races.
So will my page be colored that I write?
Being me, it will not be white.
But it will be
a part of you, instructor.
You are white—
yet a part of me, as I am a part of you.
That's American.
Sometimes perhaps you don't want to be a part of me.
Nor do I often want to be a part of you.
But we are, that's true!
As I learn from you,
I guess you learn from me—
although you're older—and white—
and somewhat more free.

This is my page for English B.

PROJECTION

n the day when the Savoy
leaps clean over to Seventh Avenue
and starts jitterbugging
with the Renaissance,
on that day when Abyssinia Baptist Church
throws her enormous arms around
St. James Presbyterian
and 409 Edgecombe
stoops to kiss 12 West 133rd,
on that day—
Do, Jesus!
Manhattan Island will whirl
like a Dizzy Gillespie transcription
played by Inez and Timme.
On that day, Lord,
Sammy Davis and Marian Anderson
will sing a duet,
Paul Robeson
will team up with Jackie Mabley,
and Father Divine will say in truth,

Peace!
It's truly
wonderful!

LATE LAST NIGHT

Late last night I
Set on my steps and cried.
Wasn't nobody gone,
Neither had nobody died.

I was cryin'
Cause you broke my heart in two.
You looked at me cross-eyed
And broke my heart in two—

So I was cryin'
On account of
You!

AS
BEFITS
A
MAN

I don't mind dying—
But I'd hate to die all alone!
I want a dozen pretty women
To holler, cry, and moan.

I don't mind dying
But I want my funeral to be fine:
A row of long tall mamas
Fainting, fanning, and crying.

I want a fish-tail hearse
And sixteen fish-tail cars,
A big brass band
And a whole truck load of flowers.

When they let me down,
Down into the clay,
I want the women to holler:
Please don't take him away!
        Ow-ooo-oo-o!
Don't take daddy away!

JUKE BOX LOVE SONG

I could take the Harlem night
and wrap around you,
Take the neon lights and make a crown,
Take the Lenox Avenue busses,
Taxis, subways,
And for your love song tone their rumble down.
Take Harlem's heartbeat,
Make a drumbeat,
Put it on a record, let it whirl,
And while we listen to it play,
Dance with you, till day—
Dance with you, my sweet brown Harlem girl.

TESTIMONIAL

If I just had a piano,
if I just had a organ,
if I just had a drum,
how I could praise my Lord!

But I don't need no piano,
       neither organ
       nor drum
for to praise my Lord!

MADAM'S CALLING

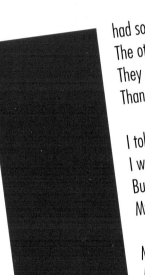

had some cards printed
The other day.
They cost me more
Than I wanted to pay.

I told the man
I wasn't no mint,
But I hankered to see
My name in print.

MADAM JOHNSON,
ALBERTA K.
He said, Your name looks good
Madam'd that way.

Shall I use Old English
Or a Roman letter?
I said, Use American.
American's better.

There's nothing foreign
To my pedigree:
Alberta K. Johnson——
American that's me.

CARDS

HARLEM
NIGHT
SONG

Come,
Let us roam the night together
Singing.

I love you.

Across
The Harlem roof-tops
Moon is shining.
Night sky is blue.
Stars are great drops
Of golden dew.

Down the street
A band is playing.

I love you.

Come,
Let us roam the night together
Singing.

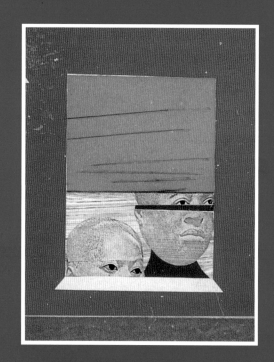

TO BE
SOMEBODY

Little girl
Dreaming of a baby grand piano
(Not knowing there's a Steinway bigger, bigger)
Dreaming of a baby grand to play
That stretches paddle-tailed across the floor,
Not standing upright
Like a bad boy in the corner,
But sending music
Up the stairs and down the stairs
And out the door
To confound even Hazel Scott
Who might be passing!

Oh!

Little boy
Dreaming of the boxing gloves
Joe Louis wore,
The gloves that sent
Two dozen men to the floor.
Knockout!
Bam! Bop! Mop!

There's always room,
They say,
At the top.

CORNER MEETING

Ladder, flag, and amplifier:
what the soap box
used to be.
The speaker catches fire
looking at their faces.
His words
jump down to stand
in listeners' places.

NOTE ON COMMERCIAL THEATRE

You've taken my blues and gone—
You sing 'em on Broadway
And you sing 'em in Hollywood Bowl,
And you mixed 'em up with symphonies
And you fixed 'em
So they don't sound like me.
Yep, you done taken my blues and gone.

You also took my spirituals and gone.
You put me in *Macbeth* and *Carmen Jones*
And all kinds of *Swing Mikados*
And in everything but what's about me—
But someday somebody'll
Stand up and talk about me,
And write about me—
Black and beautiful—
And sing about me,
And put on plays about me!
I reckon it'll be
Me myself!

Yes, it'll be me.

ST★RS

O, sweep of stars over Harlem streets,
O, little breath of oblivion that is night.
     A city building
     To a mother's song.
     A city dreaming
     To a lullaby.
Reach up your hand, dark boy, and take a star.
Out of the little breath of oblivion
     That is night,
     Take just
     One star.

ROMARE BEARDEN

Harlem was the ambience that nurtured both the life and the art of Romare Bearden. He was born in Charlotte, North Carolina, in 1911, but by the time he was three years old, his family had moved to Harlem. During his youth Bearden shuttled among New York, Baltimore, North Carolina, and Pittsburgh, where he graduated from high school. He returned to New York to attend New York University, earning a degree in mathematics. By the mid-1930s, Bearden was studying art at the Art Students League, where one of his instructors was the German artist George Grosz. At that time he also established his first studio in Harlem, at 306 West 125th Street, and became associated with the 306 Group, an informal organization that included the artists Jacob Lawrence, Norman Lewis, and Ernest Crichlow and the writers Claude McKay and Langston Hughes. It was Hughes who introduced Bearden to the work of the Spanish poet Federico García Lorca, which would become an important source of Bearden's imagery in the 1940s.

During the forties, Bearden began to exhibit his work seriously, even while serving in the United States Army (1942–45). Represented by the Samuel Kootz Gallery in New York, he also exhibited his work in several other well-established galleries, as well as in museum exhibitions in New York, Chicago, and Washington, D.C. By the sixties, Bearden's work was being shown at several galleries around the country, principally Cordier and Ekstrom Gallery. In 1950, taking advantage of educational funds made available by the G.I. Bill, Bearden studied in Paris for a year, also traveling to Italy. Upon his return to New York, he spent several years writing music while supporting himself as a caseworker for the New York City Department of Social Services. He returned to painting full time in the mid-1950s.

Bearden worked in several styles in the forties and fifties, but it was in the medium of collage that he found his signature style, first seen in works from the mid-1960s. *The Block,* created in 1971, demonstrates Bearden's deft adaptation of Cubist techniques in the depiction of space and in the disproportionate relationships among the various elements of the composition. It also shows the vitality and exuberance of Harlem, with each of the six panels presenting aspects of daily life, private or public, including neighborhood institutions such as the storefront church, the barber shop, and the corner grocery store.

The 1970s and 1980s saw the expansion of Bearden's artistic reputation. His work was exhibited widely both in the United States and abroad and is now included in numerous important private and public collections. He was in great demand as an illustrator and chronicler of African-American life and creativity, and he was awarded the National Medal of Arts award in 1987. He died in New York in 1988.

LANGSTON HUGHES

Born James Langston Hughes on February 1, 1902, in Joplin, Missouri, Hughes grew up in Kansas, Illinois, and Ohio. In his later adolescence, he spent summers in Mexico with his father. Hughes's talent for writing was recognized early: He was named class poet in the eighth grade, and he published poetry and short stories in high school. In 1921 he enrolled at Columbia University in New York, where he encountered the literary and political life of Harlem, including such individuals as Jessie Fauset, W.E.B. Du Bois, and Countee Cullen. He left school the following year, but completed his studies several years later at Lincoln University in Pennsylvania.

Hughes's biography is a chronicle of his role as a first-hand witness of some of the key events of the twentieth century: the trial of the Scottsboro boys, the formative years of the Soviet Union, the Spanish Civil War, the unfolding of the civil rights drama in the United States. Hughes met and knew most of the important political and cultural figures of his time, and his writing was informed by these extensive contacts and by his travels in Europe, Africa, the Caribbean, and the Soviet Union as well as throughout the United States. He wrote poetry, essays, novels, historical works, children's books, plays, and operatic libretti, all dealing with a wide range of issues related to African Americans and race relations, from folklore to leftist politics.

Although Langston Hughes led a peripatetic existence most of his life, it could be said that for him, as for most African Americans, Harlem was his spiritual home. Along with Countee Cullen he was considered the poet of the Harlem Renaissance. He often collaborated with the major figures of that movement, most notably with the writer Zora Neale Hurston. Hughes began to spend a great deal of time in New York after 1940, first living in the Harlem apartment of the musician Emerson Harper and his wife Toy. In 1948, he purchased a townhouse in Harlem at 20 East 127th Street. Harlem is at the heart of many of his works. *The Sweet Flypaper of Life,* published in 1955, accompanied and was inspired by photographs of Harlem by Roy De Carava. Five years later his writings served as the basis for Robert Glenn's Broadway production *Shakespeare in Harlem.* The poems in this book were originally published in the collections *One-Way Ticket* (1949), *Selected Poems* (1959), and *The Panther and the Lash* (1967).

Hughes was awarded a Rosenwald Fund fellowship in 1941 and was inducted into the National Institute of Arts and Letters in 1961. In 1966 he was appointed leader of the American delegation to the First World Festival of Negro Arts in Dakar. He died in New York in 1967.

MOTTO

I play it cool
And dig all jive.
That's the reason
I stay alive.

My motto,
As I live and learn,
    is:
*Dig And Be Dug
In Return.*